# A SMALL ★ SURPRISE

## Louise Yates

Alfred A. Knopf
New York

I
am
small.

I
am
too

small to

wipe

my

own

nose.

I am
too
small to

tie

my

own

shoes.

I am

too small to walk far

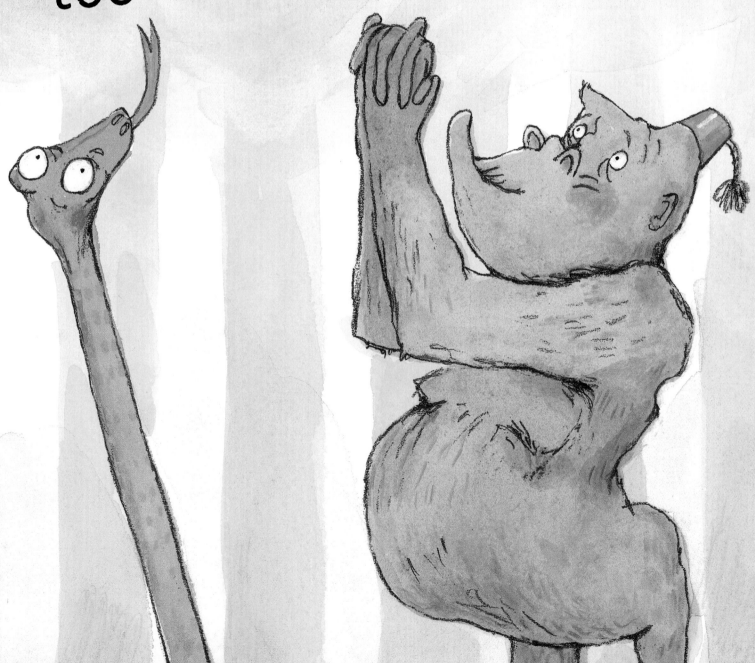

without

needing a

rest,

and

I

am

too

small

to

eat my food

without

making a mess.

But

I
am
just
the right size

to

disappear.

and  repper.

to

and

to  disappear.

and

repear.

and

that's

what

makes

me

For the people who told me
not to dedicate this to them
~ JY, AY and TD ~
a small surprise,
with love
x.

THIS IS A BORZOI BOOK PUBLISHED BY ALFRED A. KNOPF

Copyright © 2009 by Louise Yates

All rights reserved. Published in the United States by Alfred A. Knopf, an imprint of
Random House Children's Books, a division of Random House, Inc., New York.

Knopf, Borzoi Books, and the colophon are registered trademarks of Random House, Inc.
Originally published in 2009 in Great Britain by Jonathan Cape, an imprint of
Random House Children's Books.

Visit us on the Web! www.randomhouse.com/kids

Educators and librarians, for a variety of teaching tools, visit us at
www.randomhouse.com/teachers

Library of Congress Cataloging-in-Publication Data is available upon request.
ISBN 978-0-375-85698-3 (trade) — ISBN 978-0-375-95698-0 (lib. bdg.)

MANUFACTURED IN MALAYSIA
May 2009
10 9 8 7 6 5 4 3 2 1

First American Edition

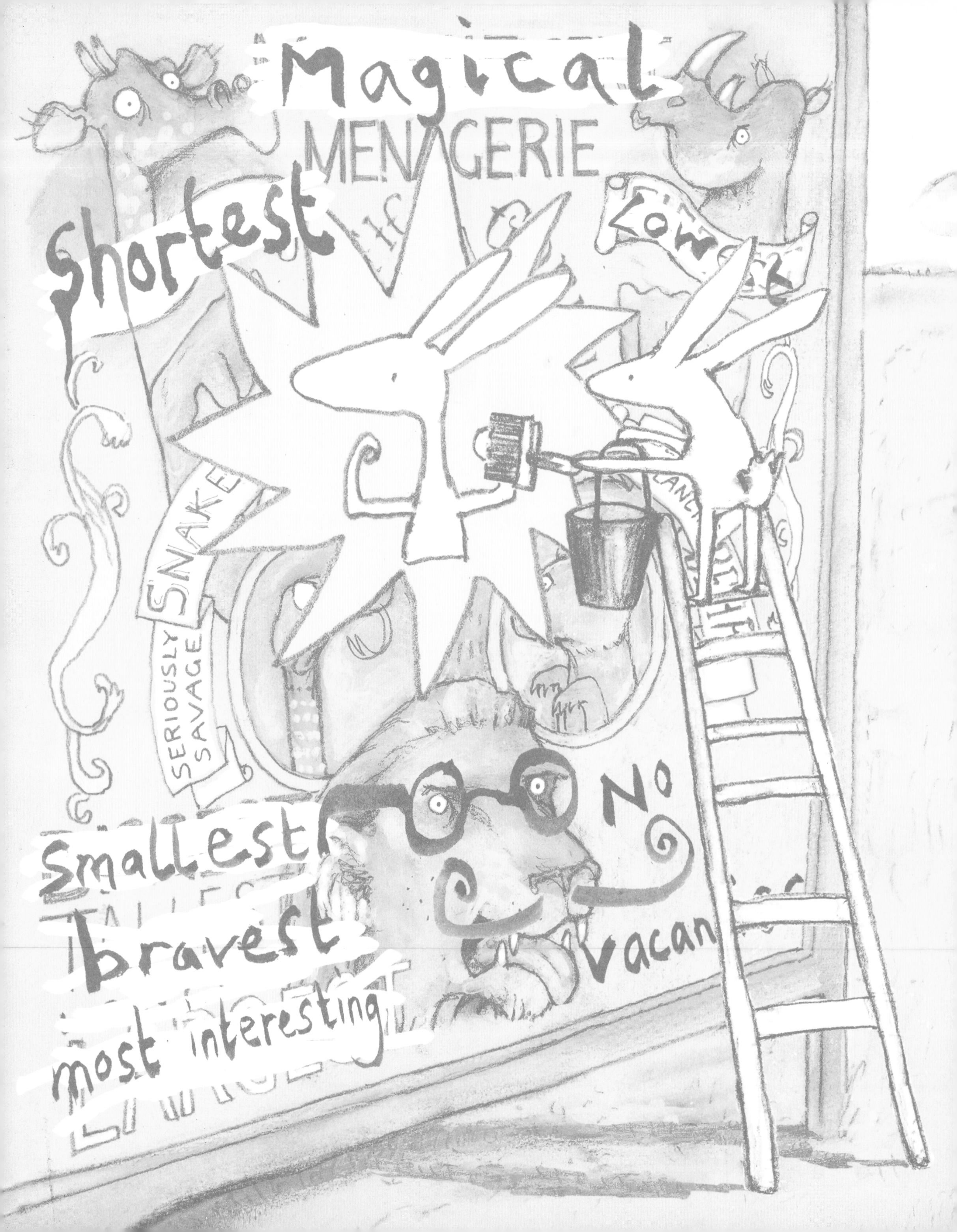